Great-Uncle Horace opened the door to the trailer and a little head peeped out. It was light brown with big, dark-brown eyes and two long, curved ears. "It's a llama!" exclaimed Zoe.

Look out for:

The Lonely Lion Cub

The Puzzled Penguin

The Playful Panda

The Silky Seal Pup

The Eager Elephant

The Lucky Snow Leopard

The Pesky Polar Bear

The Cuddly Koala

The Wild Wolf Pup

The Happy Hippo

The Sleepy Snowy Owl

The Scruffy Sea Otter

The Picky Puffin

The Giggly Giraffe

The Curious Kangaroo

The Super Sloth

Zoe's Rescue Zoo

The Little Llama

Amelia Cobb

Illustrated by
Sophy Williams

nosy crow

With special thanks to Siobhan Curham

For Sarah. Thanks for taking such good care of Zoe and her friends.

First published in the UK in 2018 by Nosy Crow Ltd
The Crow's Nest, 14 Baden Place
Crosby Row, London SE1 1YW

Nosy Crow and associated logos are trademarks and/or
registered trademarks of Nosy Crow Ltd

Text copyright © Hothouse Fiction, 2018
Illustrations © Sophy Williams, 2018

The right of Hothouse Fiction and Sophy Williams to be identified as the author
and illustrator respectively of this work has been asserted by them in accordance
with the Copyright, Designs and Patents Act 1988.

Printed and bound in Great Britain by Clays Ltd, Elcograf S.p.A.

Papers used by Nosy Crow are made from wood grown in sustainable forests.

ISBN: 978 1 78800 298 1

www.nosycrow.com

Chapter One
Very Special Guests

Zoe Parker finished her packed lunch and rushed out into the playground.

"Is it snowing yet?" called her friend Priti from behind her.

"No!" sighed Zoe. The weather forecast had been saying it might snow all week but so far there hadn't been a single flake, despite it being freezing cold. Zoe and her friends were so excited about playing in the snow! Still, Zoe did have something to look forward to. This afternoon her Great-Uncle Horace was coming to give a talk at her school. It was almost time for the school's big winter show and Great-Uncle Horace had agreed to help them with it this year!

Zoe's Great-Uncle Horace was a famous explorer and he travelled all over the world rescuing animals who were lost, injured or endangered. He brought the animals back to live at the Rescue Zoo. Zoe lived at the zoo too, with her mum, Lucy, who was the zoo vet.

"It's so cold!" said Zoe's friend Jack, coming out to join the girls. "Shall we play chase to warm up?"

"Good idea!" grinned Zoe.

But before they could begin their game she heard the sound of a car horn playing a musical tune. Zoe's eyes sparkled. There was only one car horn she knew that sounded like that and it belonged to Great-Uncle Horace! She spun round to face the school gates. Sure enough, Great-Uncle Horace's cherry-red car was pulling up outside.

"It's my great-uncle!" she cried.

"Cool car!" exclaimed Priti.

Great-Uncle Horace's car was a convertible, which meant that the roof could come down. But the roof wasn't down today because it was far too cold. A wooden trailer was attached to the back of the car. Zoe felt butterflies flutter in her tummy. Great-Uncle Horace usually used the trailer to transport animals in. Had he brought an animal with him to *school*?

"Come on, let's go and see him!" said Zoe, and she and her friends hurried over to the school gates.

The school caretaker opened the gates and Great-Uncle Horace drove inside and parked next to the playing field.

"Zoe, my dear!" he cried as he got out of the car. "It's so wonderful to see you. Brrrr, it's a bit chilly though!"

"It's so good to see you too!" said Zoe, giving him a big hug. Then she heard a weird humming sound coming from the trailer.

"What's in the trailer?" she asked.

"A special guest," replied Great-Uncle Horace with a twinkle in his eyes. "I've just collected her, so I thought I'd bring her along to join in the fun!"

4

"I thought *you* were the special guest." Zoe giggled.

"Well, yes, I suppose I am." Great-Uncle Horace grinned. "But this guest is even more special!"

The humming from the trailer grew louder. Zoe's mind raced as she tried to think what could be in there!

"I wonder what it is," said Zoe's friend Nicola.

"Maybe it's a tiger," said Priti, her eyes wide.

"Your great-uncle wouldn't bring a tiger to school," said Jack nervously. "Would he?"

Zoe laughed and shook her head.

Just then their teacher, Miss Hawkins, came hurrying over. "Mr Higgins, how lovely to see you! Welcome to the school.

The children have been so looking forward to your visit."

"Thank you, Miss Hawkins. I'm excited to see everyone too!" replied Great-Uncle Horace.

The noise from the trailer grew even louder. More and more children began gathering around the car.

"Goodness me, what is that?" asked Miss Hawkins.

Great-Uncle Horace chuckled. "I'll give you a clue. This animal has very soft wool."

"Is it a sheep?" asked Jack, looking relieved.

Zoe shook her head. "I've never heard a sheep make that noise!"

Great-Uncle Horace reached into the car and took a key from a compartment in the dashboard. "I'll give you another clue. Our special guest is one of the best climbers in the animal kingdom. She can run up the rockiest and snowiest of mountains."

Zoe wracked her brains trying to think of what it could be. "Is it a mountain goat?"

Great-Uncle Horace shook his head. He took the key over to the trailer and unlocked the door. "Are you ready?"

"Yes!" chorused the children, apart from Jack, who was still looking a bit nervous.

Great-Uncle Horace opened the door to the trailer and a little head peeped out. It was light brown with big, dark-brown eyes and two long, curved ears.

"It's a llama!" exclaimed Zoe.

"Correct!" replied Great-Uncle Horace.

The llama stepped out of the trailer and looked around curiously. Its golden-brown wool was so soft and fluffy Zoe instantly wanted to cuddle it.

"It's so cute!" said Priti.

The little llama looked at all the children gathered around and let out another humming sound.

"Do you think she's saying hello?" asked Nicola.

Zoe nodded. But she didn't just *think* the llama was saying hello, she *knew* she was! Zoe had a special secret that nobody, not even Great-Uncle Horace, knew about. She could speak to animals and understand what they were saying!

"Hello," she said, stroking the little

llama under her chin.

The llama nuzzled her hand, then started gently butting her with her head.

"What's she doing?" Priti giggled as the llama started butting her too.

"She's saying hello and trying to herd you," replied Great-Uncle Horace with a chortle. "Llamas are very sociable animals. Farmers often use them to take care of their other animals, like sheep and goats."

"Shall we go inside where it's warmer?" said Miss Hawkins.

"Yes, the poor llama must be freezing." Nicola pulled her woolly hat down over her ears.

"Oh, she'll be OK," said Great-Uncle Horace. "Llamas come from the mountains in South America. They're used to the cold. I, however, do not come from the mountains, and I would love to get into the warm." He rubbed his hands together.

Just then there was a loud squawk

from the car
and Kiki, a
beautiful hyacinth
macaw, flew out
and perched on
Great-Uncle Horace's
shoulder. Kiki travelled
everywhere with
Great-Uncle Horace.
She didn't like the
cold weather either!

"Come on," said Miss Hawkins. "I'll
make you a nice cup of tea."

"Wonderful!" Great-Uncle Horace took
a lead from his coat pocket and put it
around the llama's neck. Then he handed
the lead to Zoe. "Could you hold her
for a moment, Zoe? I just need to get
something."

"Of course." Zoe felt very proud as she held the lead tightly. She wanted to be a zookeeper when she grew up, so she loved helping out with the Rescue Zoo animals whenever she could.

Great-Uncle Horace came back a moment later with a bag of llama food pellets in one hand and a packet of biscuits in the other. Zoe grinned. Great-Uncle Horace never went anywhere without his beloved custard creams!

Miss Hawkins led them all into the school hall, where the other children were sitting down. The little llama kept tugging on her lead, trying to nuzzle all the children, but Zoe kept a tight grip.

Once they were all settled, Great-Uncle Horace got up on the stage, holding his cup of tea and biscuits. Kiki settled down on the back of a chair and started to preen her beautiful blue feathers.

First, Miss Hawkins introduced Great-Uncle Horace to everyone. "Now, children, it'll soon be time for our end-of-term school show. As you all know, this year the theme is 'Our Wintry World'. The performance will be all about the colder parts of our planet and the animals that live there."

Miss Hawkins paused and smiled at the children. "Now for some exciting news! Mr Higgins is going to help to make our show extra special this year. He has agreed that some of the zoo animals that come from cold areas of the world can be part of our show!"

At this news the children started cheering and chatting among themselves.

Zoe gave a huge smile. She was so excited that the Rescue Zoo and her school would be working together! She couldn't wait to help choose animals to star in the show.

Great-Uncle Horace smiled at Miss Hawkins and waved at the children. "Hello, everyone!" he said, his voice booming around the hall. "It is a great honour to be here, and to be helping you with your winter show! First, I'll tell you a bit more about the Rescue Zoo.

"Well, *the* most important job we do is looking after animals who don't have a suitable or safe home. We take good care of them and make sure they are healthy and happy. And today I've brought our latest arrival along to meet you all!" He pointed to the front of the hall, where

Zoe was standing next to the llama. "Zoe, would you like to bring her up on to the stage?"

Zoe led the llama on to the stage and over to Great-Uncle Horace. The llama nuzzled his arm.

"I collected this little llama just this morning," continued Great-Uncle Horace, "and I hope she will be very happy with us at the Rescue Zoo."

Jack put his hand up.

"Yes, young man?" said Great-Uncle Horace.

"Why did you have to rescue her?" asked Jack.

"She'd been abandoned by her owner," replied Great-Uncle Horace sadly. "Someone reported seeing her all alone on a piece of wasteland, and the authorities asked if I'd take her in."

"At least she'll be well looked after now, at the zoo," said Jack.

"Yes, she will." Great-Uncle Horace smiled. "And it will be lovely having a llama about the place. They're very friendly creatures. Even when they get angry or feel under threat they don't bite or attack – they just spit!"

The children started to giggle.

"Llamas are also herd animals, which means they like to live with other llamas." His smile faded a little. "Unfortunately we don't have any other llamas at the zoo. So, for now, we'll have to think of a clever way to give her some company and keep her happy."

Zoe stroked the llama's soft wool. She hated thinking of her without any llama friends.

Just then Zoe had a brilliant idea. Perhaps the little llama could star in the

school show? After all, Great-Uncle
Horace had said that llamas live in the
mountains of South America where
it is often very cold. And Zoe and her
classmates had been learning all about
South America. She decided she would
speak to Great-Uncle Horace about it
later.

As the children cheered and chattered
excitedly about the show, Zoe hugged the
llama to her. This was turning into the
best day ever. Not only did she have a
new animal friend to get to know but she
and her schoolmates would be putting on
a *very* special winter show!

Chapter Two
Herd Hunting

As soon as the bell rang for the end of school, Zoe rushed outside. She couldn't wait to get back home and spend more time with the little llama.

Zoe's mum Lucy was waiting for her by the school gates, wearing her Rescue Zoo vet's uniform.

All the way down the road Zoe talked

to her mum about the show and how
she hoped the new little llama might be
able to star in it. Her mum agreed it was
a good idea, as long as the llama settled
in well over the next few days. As they
approached the zoo they passed some
visitors who were just leaving.

"That tiny lemur was so funny," Zoe
overhead one of them say. She grinned.
There was only one tiny lemur they could
be talking about – Meep! She wondered
what her cheeky little friend had done
this time.

As Zoe and Lucy walked through the
zoo gates Zoe saw a flash of grey fur.
Meep was scampering up the carvings of
flamingos and giraffes and parrots right
to the very top of the gates, where he
perched on top of the carving of a hot-air

balloon. It was a model of the real hot-
air balloon that belonged to Great-Uncle
Horace — it was his favourite way to
travel the world. Zoe looked up at Meep
and laughed.

"Look at Meep, Mum."

Lucy looked up at Meep and smiled.
"It's so sweet that he's always here,
waiting for you to get home."

Meep scampered down the gate and
leapt into Zoe's arms.

"Right, I need to pop back to the
hospital," said Lucy. "Poor Chi Chi got a
splinter in her paw."

"Oh no!" said Zoe. "Will she be OK?"
Chi Chi was one of the Rescue Zoo
pandas. Great-Uncle Horace had brought
her and her sister Mei Mei to the zoo
when they were just cubs.

22

"She'll be fine," replied Lucy. "You head back to the cottage. Great-Uncle Horace is waiting there for you."

Lucy headed off to the hospital while Zoe and Meep hurried along the path that led to their cottage.

"You'll never guess what, Meep. Great-Uncle Horace has rescued a llama and he brought it to our school!"

"Llama sounds just like lemur," chattered Meep. "Does it look like me, Zoe?"

Zoe chuckled. "No. She's a lot bigger and woollier than you, Meep." She wondered which enclosure Great-Uncle Horace had put the llama in. Hopefully she'd be able to go and visit her soon and find out all about her.

When they got to the cottage Zoe

23

heard a humming sound coming from the back garden. She let herself in, dumped her school bag on the floor and went straight to the garden to investigate.

To her surprise, Great-Uncle Horace was standing in the middle of the garden and the llama was circling him and jumping around playfully!

"Aha!" he cried when he saw Zoe. "We've been waiting for you to get back. I need your help with something. Well, two things, actually."

"Cool!" said Zoe. She was so excited that the little llama was in her garden!

"Firstly, our new arrival needs a name, and as you're so good at coming up with names for the animals, I thought you ought to choose one."

Zoe bit her lip to stop from giggling.

Little did he know that she hardly ever came up with the animals' names herself. She just pretended she had after they *told* her what they were called.

"Yes, of course," she replied.

"Thank you! And secondly, I need you to help me find our new arrival some animal friends to live with for the time being. She really needs a herd to make her happy." The llama trotted up to Meep and Zoe and nudged them with her head until they stood next to Great-Uncle Horace. "See!" he chuckled. "She's trying to make us part of her herd!"

"That's so sweet!" exclaimed Zoe.

"I'll just go and get her lead and then we'll set off," said Great-Uncle Horace. "I thought we could try her with the goats first."

As soon as he'd gone back inside the cottage Zoe and Meep went over to the llama.

"Hello again," said Zoe. "Welcome to the Rescue Zoo."

The llama nuzzled Zoe's hand, then she slowly and carefully lowered her head and gently nuzzled Meep.

"Hello," chattered Meep. "My name's Meep and I'm a lemur, which sounds just like llama, but actually we're very different."

"And my name's Zoe," said Zoe. "What's your name?"

The llama made a little barking sound.

"What a lovely name!" exclaimed Zoe. "Hello, Lottie."

Lottie the llama started nudging Zoe on the arm until she stood right next to Meep.

"What's she doing?" Meep giggled.

"I think she's trying to herd me,"
explained Zoe. "Llamas love to look
after other animals. They're a bit like
sheepdogs."

Lottie trotted in a circle around them.

"But we're not sheep!" exclaimed Meep.
"Even though my name sounds like sheep.
Meep the sheep," he chattered.

"I know. That's why we need to find her
some animals to live with," replied Zoe.

Just then a face popped over the garden
fence. A rather grumpy face. It belonged
to Mr Pinch, the zoo manager.

"What on earth is going on here?" said
Mr Pinch as Lottie bounced around Zoe
and Meep.

"Hello, Mr Pinch. This is Lottie the llama.
Great-Uncle Horace just rescued her."

"What is she doing in your garden?"
Mr Pinch frowned. "Why isn't she in an
enclosure?"

"Don't worry," said Zoe. "We're about
to find her a place to stay."

To Zoe's relief, Great-Uncle Horace reappeared, holding a lead.

"Good afternoon, Mr Pinch!" he boomed. "And how are you this wonderful winter's day?"

"I don't see what's so wonderful about it, Horace," grumbled Mr Pinch. "It's freezing cold and there's a bouncing animal loose in this garden."

"Don't worry," replied Great-Uncle Horace. "We're about to remove this little llama from the garden and find her a proper home."

"Glad to hear it!" replied Mr Pinch. "Anyway, I can't stand around having conversations over fences all day. I have work to do."

Mr Pinch's face disappeared and Zoe sighed. Mr Pinch could be such a misery!

"Right, are you ready?" asked Great-Uncle Horace.

Zoe nodded.

"And did you think of a name for her?"

"Yes. She's called Lottie."

"Lottie the llama. Excellent choice."

Zoe looked at Lottie and grinned.

Zoe, Great-Uncle Horace, Lottie and Meep set off along the path that wound through the middle of the zoo. It was almost dark and the old-fashioned lamps had come on, casting a golden glow on the cobblestones. The petting zoo where the goats lived was in the middle of the zoo, behind the café and gift shop. There were three goats at the zoo and Zoe really hoped they'd want to be Lottie's friends. As they turned the corner behind the gift shop, Tony, the keeper in charge of the petting zoo, appeared from the pigsties holding a broom and a bucket.

"Hello!" he called cheerfully. "Who do you have there, Mr Higgins?"

"Good afternoon, Tony," said Great-Uncle Horace. "This is Lottie the llama. She's looking for a herd. Would it be OK if we tried her in with the goats?"

"Of course," replied Tony. "I've just fed them their dinner, so they should be happy and relaxed!"

"Thank you. Could you open the gate, please, Zoe?" asked Great-Uncle Horace.

Zoe felt for the pendant around her neck. It was silver and in the shape of a paw-print. Great-Uncle Horace had given it to her as a special birthday present and it opened all of the zoo enclosures. She pressed the pendant to

a panel next to the
gate and it swung
open. One of
the goats came
trotting over.
Zoe patted her
on the head.

"Hello, Greta,
we've got a new
friend for you,"
she said.

Great-Uncle Horace led Lottie into the
enclosure. The other goats came trotting
over and the animals gave each other an
inquisitive sniff. Lottie was only a little bit
bigger than the goats!

"So far, so good," said Great-Uncle
Horace, letting Lottie off her lead.

"She's a beauty," said Tony, as Lottie

started bouncing around the enclosure.

"She certainly is," replied Great-Uncle Horace.

Then Lottie started nudging the goats with her head. But the goats didn't want to move, and Greta gave a cross grunt.

"Uh-oh!" chattered Meep, scampering up on to Zoe's shoulder.

Lottie butted another of the goats with her head. Greta grunted again, then she butted Lottie back, almost knocking her over.

"I don't think the goats like being herded," said Zoe.

"I think you're right," replied Great-Uncle Horace.

Lottie made a loud warbling noise and trotted around the goats again, trying to get them to move into the centre of the enclosure. But the goats ran off into their shed, bleating. Lottie stood all alone in the middle of the enclosure looking very sad.

"Oh dear," said Great-Uncle Horace, scratching his head. "That didn't work out quite as I'd hoped. Well, let's try the pigs next!"

The Rescue Zoo kunekune pigs were very friendly. They had thick fur, a bit like Lottie's, and liked to eat grass. Zoe felt sure they would get on well with the little llama!

"Hello, Percy, hello Polly," said Zoe as she opened the gate to their enclosure.

The pigs grunted a greeting as Lottie

trotted over to them and hummed happily.

The pigs continued lying there. They had just had their dinner and were enjoying their nap.

Lottie hummed louder and nudged each one with her nose. The pigs didn't move and Lottie came back over to Zoe.

"Pigs don't really do much, I'm afraid," whispered Zoe, patting the little llama on her head.

Lottie brayed sadly. Zoe knew she was saying that she wanted someone to play with *and* look after!

Chapter Three
Donkey Disaster!

"Oh dear," said Great-Uncle Horace
thoughtfully, as they walked Lottie out
of the pigsty. "She wasn't very happy
there either, was she? Well, perhaps we
should sleep on it tonight and try again
tomorrow with some other animals."

"But where will she stay tonight?" asked
Zoe.

"We'll ask your mum if she can stay in your garden," said Great-Uncle Horace. "If she says yes I'll ask Tony if he can quickly put up a temporary shelter so Lottie will be warm and dry."

Zoe smiled. "Can I walk her back home?"

"Certainly." Great-Uncle Horace handed her the lead.

As Great-Uncle Horace called Zoe's mum on the phone, Zoe went over to Lottie and hugged her close. "Don't worry," she whispered into the llama's long, curved ear. "We'll find you some animals to live with soon, but until then, Meep and I can be your herd."

Meep chattered in agreement and Lottie gave a contented hum.

As soon as Zoe woke up the next morning, she looked out of her bedroom window into the back garden. Tony had built Lottie a small temporary shelter out of some spare planks of wood, to make sure the little llama would be snug and warm during the night. But Lottie wasn't in the shelter! She was over by Zoe's mum's favourite rose bush, nibbling on the leaves. Zoe gently nudged Meep, who was curled up asleep at the end of her bed.

"Wake up, Meep. Lottie's eating Mum's rose bush!"

Meep rubbed his eyes with his paws sleepily. "Why's she eating the rose bush?"

"She must be hungry." Zoe put a jumper on over her pyjamas. "Let's go and get her some breakfast."

"Breakfast!" Meep sprang from the bed,

all of his sleepiness suddenly gone. Zoe grinned. Breakfast was one of Meep's most favourite things in the world . . . and so were lunch and dinner!

As Zoe and Meep hurried out on to the landing, Lucy was just coming out of her bedroom, wearing her dressing gown and yawning. "Where are you two going in such a hurry?" she asked.

"We're just going to check on Lottie in the garden," replied Zoe.

"To stop her eating the garden!" chattered Meep, sliding down the banister.

Zoe was really glad Lucy couldn't understand what the little lemur was saying. She didn't want to get Lottie into trouble!

"Well, don't stay out there too long, it's freezing," said Lucy, heading into the bathroom.

"We won't," called Zoe as she raced down the stairs.

Zoe put on her coat and shoes and poured some of the pellets Great-Uncle Horace had left for Lottie into a bowl. Then she and Meep went into the garden. It was freezing cold and the frost-covered grass crunched under her feet. When Lottie saw them, she gave an excited bray and came trotting over. She gently nuzzled Zoe, then bent her head down and gave Meep an extra-gentle nuzzle.

"Good morning, Lottie. We've brought you some breakfast," said Zoe, placing the bowl down in front of her.

Lottie hummed contentedly.

"You're welcome!" Zoe stroked her soft woolly coat.

The Little Llama

"I'm hungry," said Meep, watching enviously as Lottie began to eat.

Zoe grinned. Meep was always hungry! "I'll get you some breakfast in a minute," she said.

"Lottie's ears look just like bananas," said Meep. "Delicious, big bananas." He gave a huge sigh.

Zoe looked at Lottie. Meep was right. Her ears were curved just like bananas!

Zoe laughed. "All right, come on, let's go and get some breakfast. We'll be back soon, Lottie."

Just as they got back to the kitchen there was a knock on the front door.

"Hello! Is anyone up?" boomed a voice through the letterbox.

"Great-Uncle Horace!" Zoe ran to open the door.

"Good morning, Zoe!" Great-Uncle Horace came striding in. He was wearing his long winter coat and a matching stripy bobble hat and scarf. "How's our little llama friend doing?"

"Great. I just gave her some breakfast," replied Zoe.

"Excellent! And speaking of breakfast. . ." he grinned. "Who's for some blueberry pancakes?"

Meep jumped up and down excitedly.

Great-Uncle Horace fetched a bowl from the cupboard. "Zoe, I had a call from your teacher last night. She's very keen that we choose some suitable animals to star in the show."

"Great!" smiled Zoe. She knew that once the special wintry animals had been chosen, Miss Hawkins and the rest of the class would be able to plan the rest of the show. There was only a week to go until the end of term, so there was no time to waste!

Great-Uncle Horace poured some flour into the bowl to make the pancake batter. "Well, perhaps some of your class could come to the zoo this weekend to help us choose which animals should be in the show?"

"That would be brilliant!" smiled Zoe. "I thought Lottie might be a good choice to star in the show too, as she's friendly and comes from the cold mountains?"

"Good idea, Zoe!" replied Great-Uncle Horace, stirring the pancake batter.

Zoe grinned. Now she had lots of things to look forward to. Finding Lottie a herd *and* choosing more animals for the winter-themed show!

After school that day, Great-Uncle Horace, Zoe and Meep took Lottie to the donkey enclosure.

"Hopefully Dora and Danny will be the perfect llama companions," said Great-Uncle Horace, as Zoe pressed her pendant to the gate and they let Lottie in.

The two donkeys came trotting over. Zoe took a couple of carrots from her coat pocket.

"Hello, Dora. Hello, Danny. This is Lottie," said Zoe, holding the carrots out to them.

The donkeys gave Lottie a welcoming bray, before nibbling on their carrots.

Lottie trotted around the enclosure, making soft humming sounds. She

bounced up to Danny and gave him
a nudge with her head. She was much
smaller than him, but the nudge still made
him drop his carrot. Danny put his ears
back and gave Lottie a warning bray. She

trotted away, looking sad, and stood by herself with her head hanging down.

Great-Uncle Horace sighed. "Oh dear. I'm not sure this is going to work!"

Zoe thought for a moment. "Great-Uncle Horace, would it be OK if Lottie stays in the cottage garden for the time being?"

"I don't see why not," replied Great-Uncle Horace. "To be perfectly honest, I'm not sure what other animals to try next. She really needs some llamas to spend time with."

Zoe went back over to Lottie. "Don't worry, Meep and I are proud to be part of your herd," she whispered. Lottie snuggled up to Zoe and she gave the little animal a big hug. Meep jumped on Lottie's back and flung his arms around her neck. Lottie looked a bit happier, but Zoe knew she *really* wanted some special llama friends.

Chapter Four
Stars of the Show

On Saturday morning Zoe woke up extra early feeling very excited. At school on Friday Miss Hawkins had picked five names out of a hat, so today Jack, Elliot, Priti, Grace and Mark were coming to the zoo to help choose animals for the show!

As soon as she, Meep and Lottie had

had their breakfast Zoe packed her bag
with a notepad and pen. Great-Uncle
Horace had put her in charge of writing
the list of animals she and her friends
wanted for the show. Then she sat and
watched the clock on the kitchen wall as
its hands slowly ticked closer to the time
when her friends would arrive. When
Lucy came into the kitchen and saw her
she started to laugh.

"Time won't go any faster if you watch
it."

"I know!" Zoe sighed. "It seems to go
even slower!"

"Why don't you go and get Lottie
ready?" suggested Lucy.

"Ready for what?"

"To take with you. Great-Uncle Horace
just called and said she could probably do

with some exercise."

"Yay!" cheered Zoe, leaping up from her seat. Meep ran around in a circle on the table.

By the time Zoe had given Lottie something to eat and put on her lead it was time to go and meet her friends. Although it was still early, the zoo was already filling with visitors, wrapped up warm in the winter sunshine. They all smiled when they saw Zoe making her way along the winding footpath with Meep perched on her shoulder and little Lottie on her lead.

When they got to the zoo gates Priti was already waiting there with her mum.

"Hey, Zoe," she cried. "Hello, Meep. Hello, Lottie." She gave Zoe a hug and patted Lottie and Meep. "You're so lucky to live at a zoo! It must be so much fun!"

"It is," agreed Zoe. Then she had a brilliant idea. "I know, why don't I ask my mum if you can come for a sleepover one night? Then you can see what it's like."

Priti's eyes grew wide with excitement. "Oh, yes, please." She turned to her mum. "Would that be OK, Mum?"

Priti's mum nodded and smiled. "Of course! I'll chat to Zoe's mum today if you like and see what she says."

Both girls nodded and Priti gave Zoe's hands an excited squeeze.

Just then Elliot and Jack arrived with their parents, followed by Mark and Grace.

"Good morning! Good morning!" boomed Great-Uncle Horace, striding over, his long scarf flapping behind him in the breeze. "Welcome to the Rescue Zoo!"

Once the parents had left, the children all gathered round Lottie and petted her.

"Great-Uncle Horace said that she can come with us to look at the animals as she needs to get some exercise," explained Zoe.

"I have to make some urgent repairs to my hot-air balloon, so Zoe will be your tour guide," said Great-Uncle Horace. "She can show you all the animals that come from cold climates, and when you've agreed your list of animal co-stars I'll meet you in the café for some hot chocolate and cake. I don't know about you, but I've always found that meetings are so much more fun when there's hot chocolate and cake!"

The children all giggled and nodded.

"Farewell for now," said Great-Uncle Horace, turning to go. "Or, as they say in the Andes, *huq ratukama!*"

"Your great-uncle's so cool!" exclaimed Elliot as they watched him striding off down the path. As he passed by each enclosure the animals chirped, roared and trumpeted excited greetings. If it wasn't for Great-Uncle Horace, they wouldn't have such a great home. They all loved him very much.

Zoe grinned. "Yes, he's the best!"

Holding Lottie tightly on her lead, Zoe led her friends along the path that went around the edge of the zoo. The hippo enclosure was the first they came to. Henry the hippo was splashing happily in the muddy pond at the centre of the

enclosure. When
he saw
Zoe, he
threw
back his
huge head
and grunted
a greeting.

"Hello,
Henry!"
called Zoe.

"Can we have a hippo in our show?"
asked Mark hopefully.

"I don't think so," said Zoe. "Hippos
live in Africa, where it's usually nice and
warm."

"Plus, if we had a hippo there wouldn't
be room for anyone else on the stage,"
grinned Grace.

The next enclosure belonged to the polar bears. Bella, the oldest polar bear, was climbing one of the wooden frames in the play area outside their huge igloo. Zoe hoped the polar bears would have some snow to play in soon. They were one of the few animals at the zoo who were actually used to the weather being so cold!

"What about a polar bear?" asked Nicola.

"It's a good idea, but I think they might be a bit too big now," replied Zoe.

Just then Snowy came out of the igloo and looked around. Zoe smiled as she remembered how small the bear had been when Great-Uncle Horace first brought her to the zoo. She'd been the perfect size for the show back then but now she was

almost fully grown. Snowy and her friend
Bella lumbered over to the enclosure
fence and barked happily.

"Maybe we need to go and see some of
the smaller animals," said Grace.

"Good idea."
Zoe led them
round the
corner to
the penguin
enclosure. The
penguins had
all gathered on the
huge pale-blue iceberg
in the middle of their
lagoon. It shimmered
like a jewel
in the pale
winter

sunshine. When the penguins saw Zoe
and her friends they splashed down into
the water and swam over to them.

"Aw, they're so cute," said Priti as one
by one the penguins waddled out of the
water and across the bank to greet them.

"Please can we have some penguins in
the show?" asked Nicola. "They usually
live in cool parts of the world, don't they?"

"Good idea!" Zoe knew just which
penguin would enjoy the show the most.
She took her notepad and pen from her
bag and wrote "PIP THE PENGUIN and
friends" at the top of the page. "Hello,
Pip," she said as one of the penguins came
waddling up to the glass wall.

Zoe couldn't help grinning as she
remembered back to the time when Pip
had first arrived at the zoo. The little

chick had been convinced he wasn't a
penguin. At one point he'd even thought
he was a flamingo! Zoe and Pip had
become very good friends.

Just then they heard a loud trumpeting
sound from the enclosure next door. They
turned to see Oscar the elephant waving
his trunk in the air. Zoe knew he was
saying that he wanted to be in the show
too! But he'd be much too big . . . *and*
elephants didn't live in cold climates!

Next, the six classmates went to the
snow leopard enclosure. Ali came up to
the fence to say hello, followed closely by
his three little sisters, Holly, Snowy and
Ivy. Although the three sisters were no
longer tiny cubs they were still quite little
and very friendly, and Zoe thought that
they would be perfect for the show.

"They're adorable!" cried Elliot. "Please can the cubs be in the school show?"

"That would be great, but we'll have to check with Matt, the big-cat keeper," explained Zoe. "The cubs are very friendly, but they have very sharp teeth and we don't want anyone to get nibbled!" She wrote down "SNOW LEOPARD CUBS?" in her notebook.

Next, Zoe took her friends to the puffin enclosure. Puffins lived in lots of different places, including the Arctic, where it was freezing cold. When Meep saw Piper coming out of her burrow he started hopping about happily. Zoe grinned. It was funny thinking of how jealous Meep had been when Piper first arrived at the zoo. Now they were great friends, and Piper had five puffin pals too! Just then Rory the puffin keeper came out of the shed beside the enclosure holding a bucket of fish.

"Morning, Zoe," he called when he saw her.

"Morning, Rory," replied Zoe. "These are some of my friends from school. I was wondering if you could show them how good Piper is at catching fish?"

"Of course," replied Rory. He went into the enclosure, took a shiny silver fish from the bucket and threw it high in the air.

Piper opened her beak and caught it expertly.

"Cool!" exclaimed Priti, and the other children cheered. Even Mark looked impressed.

"We definitely need her in the show," said Elliot.

Zoe grinned and added "PIPER THE PUFFIN and pals" to her list.

A little while later, after visiting lots of other animals, the friends headed to the

café, where Great-Uncle Horace was
waiting for them at a table outside.

"Welcome!" he cried, gesturing at them
to join him. "How did you get on?"

"Great," replied Zoe. "We have our list
to show you." She carefully tied Lottie's
lead to a chair leg and sat down.

Sally, who ran the café, came over
holding her notepad and pen. "What can
I get you?" she asked with a cheery grin.

"Hot chocolates and rice crispy cakes
all round," smiled Great-Uncle Horace.

"Of course," replied Sally. She jotted the
order in her notepad and went hurrying
back inside.

"So," said Great-Uncle Horace, "who
have you chosen to star in your show?"

Zoe took her list from her bag. "Pip
the penguin and friends, Piper the puffin

and pals, Holly, Snowy and Ivy the snow leopard cubs if possible, Oscar the snowy owl and his mate Shelley, and, of course, Lottie the llama."

"Excellent list!" exclaimed Great-Uncle Horace. "I'm sure Matt the big-cat keeper will be OK for the snow leopard cubs to appear in the show. After all, he and the other zoo keepers will be looking after the animals to make sure they are all happy and behaving themselves."

Sally returned with a tray full of steaming hot chocolates, topped with whipped cream and marshmallows.

Zoe took a sip of her drink. It was delicious. She patted Lottie on the head. She couldn't help but notice that she looked a little sad. Zoe untied her lead and took her away from the group, so she could find out what was wrong.

"Are you OK, Lottie?" she whispered.

The little llama hummed softly in reply.

"You want to be in the show with your friends?" repeated Zoe. Then she realised that all of the other animals would be on stage with their family or friends . . . and Lottie would be by herself.

"Oh! But you'll be with all of us!" whispered Zoe, stroking Lottie's soft ears.

But Lottie still looked very sad.

Chapter Five
Planning the Winter Show

On Monday the class finalised their plans for the winter show. Miss Hawkins had divided the class into five groups, each one named after the five animals chosen for the show: penguin, puffin, snow leopard, llama and snowy owl. Each group had spent the morning researching their animal and the different parts of the world they lived in.

Miss Hawkins smiled at the class and clapped her hands. "Each group has ten minutes to come up with ideas for a performance all about their animal and where they live in the wild. Off you go!"

All of the children started chattering excitedly. Everyone had lots of ideas! Zoe was in the llama group and she enjoyed telling her friends all she knew about Lottie and her relatives in the wild. After ten minutes had passed, Miss Hawkins clapped her hands and one person from each group called out their suggestions.

"We'd like to read out a funny poem about penguins," called Elliot.

"Great idea!" nodded Miss Hawkins, writing down "PENGUIN POEM" on the whiteboard.

"We'd like to make a HUGE map to hold up, showing where snowy owls live in North America and Canada, and use pictures to show where the owls live at different times of the year!" cried Eve, grinning excitedly.

"Wonderful!" smiled Miss Hawkins, jotting it down. Soon the plan for the performance was finalised! Zoe's llama group had decided to dress up as llamas, with long furry ears. They would read out some fascinating facts about llamas and where they live and sing a special llama song.

As each group performed, the animals would be brought on to the stage so everyone in the audience could see them. Then the class would sing a song together. Zoe couldn't wait!

After a busy week making props and banners for the show, at last it was Wednesday afternoon. Only two days to go until the show! That night something very exciting was happening... Priti was coming for a sleepover! Priti was in Zoe's llama group and they were planning to spend the evening making furry llama ears for their group to wear during the show. The very next day the whole class was coming to the zoo for a dress rehearsal of the performance, and the animals would join in too!

As the girls hurried out of school hand in hand Zoe felt something icy land on the tip of her nose. She looked up and let out a cheer. Snowflakes were fluttering from the sky like white feathers. "It's

snowing! At last!"

"Yay!" cried Priti.

All the way back to the zoo the girls chatted excitedly to Lucy about the show.

"We're learning so many amazing things about llamas!" exclaimed Zoe. "Can we take Lottie for a little walk around the zoo when we get back?"

"Of course," agreed Lucy. "She'll

probably enjoy the snow! And Great-
Uncle Horace asked if you would help
him prepare the zebras for the night to
make sure they stay nice and warm. You
could take Lottie along with you."

"OK," said Zoe.

Priti looked at her and grinned. "This
sleepover is going to be so much fun!"

Meep wasn't perched on the Rescue
Zoo gates this time. Zoe had asked him
to stay in the cottage garden to keep
Lottie company. As they followed the path
round to the cottage Zoe heard Lottie's
loud bray, followed by Meep's chattering.

"Sounds like someone's having fun," said
Lucy.

While Lucy made the girls something to
eat, Zoe took Priti into the back garden.
Lottie was bouncing round in circles

looking very happy. Meep was standing in the centre of the garden, his tail drooping and his eyes closed. He looked really tired. As soon as he saw Zoe he came scampering over.

"Hello, Meep." Zoe picked up the little lemur and cuddled him to her.

"Oh, Zoe, I'm so tired!" he chattered quietly. "Lottie has been bouncing around all day! She's been herding me all over the place and telling me where to go. She even tried to groom me and get me to eat some grass . . . yuck!"

As Priti went over to pet Lottie, Zoe whispered in Meep's ear. "Don't worry, we're going to take Lottie out now to see the zebras."

Meep breathed a sigh of relief. "I really like Lottie," he chattered, "but it's hard work being in her herd!"

Lottie came trotting over and nuzzled Zoe. Some snowflakes had landed in her fluffy woollen coat and they glistened like stars in the light from the cottage.

"Hello, Lottie," said Zoe, patting the little llama on the head. "We're going to take you out now, to see some zebras."

Lottie brayed excitedly and ran around in a circle to celebrate.

Once the girls had got changed out of their school uniforms Zoe put Lottie on her lead and they set off for the zebra enclosure. It was snowing heavily now and the flakes shone gold in the pools of light from the old-fashioned lamps. The zebras lived in a forest area at the far end of the zoo. When they got to the arched wooden doorway leading to the enclosure

Zoe placed her paw-print pendant on the panel next to it and it swung open.

"Wow!" said Priti as they walked inside. "It's like being in an enchanted forest."

Zoe grinned. Priti was right, and the enclosure looked even more magical now the chestnut trees were dusted in snowflakes. She heard the soft thud of hooves on the ground and turned to see one of the

zebras, Cleo, trotting towards them.

"Hello, Cleo," called Zoe as the zebra whinnied a greeting.

Cleo looked at Lottie curiously.

"This is Lottie the llama," said Zoe.

Lottie gave Cleo a cheery bray.

"It's like they're saying hello to each other." Priti giggled.

Zoe grinned. She wished Priti was able to understand animals too. Then she'd know that they *were* saying hello to each other!

"I wonder where Great-Uncle Horace is," said Zoe as they started making their way through the trees.

"He's right here!" declared Great-Uncle Horace, appearing through the snow. He was wearing his long winter coat and holding a bundle of blankets. "Thank you for coming to help me."

The girls and Lottie, Meep and Cleo all followed Great-Uncle Horace through the

forest. Finally they got to the stable where the zebras slept at night. At the sound of their voices Theo, the other Rescue Zoo zebra, came trotting out of the stable.

"OK, girls, let's get the zebras' bedroom cosy for the night," said Great-Uncle Horace.

Zoe and Priti followed him into the stable. There was a huge pile of hay in the middle of the floor and two heaters stood against the wall.

"Could you move the hay over to

the corner, please?" asked Great-Uncle Horace, handing the girls a large fork each. "And I'll see to these." He nodded to the heaters.

"Do all of the animals need heaters in the cold?" asked Priti.

Great-Uncle Horace shook his head. "No, only the ones who come from hot climates. Zebras come from Africa originally, so they're really not built for this kind of weather. The polar bears, on the other hand, are enjoying the cold very much!"

Zoe grinned as she thought of Snowy and Bella having fun in the snow.

There was a sudden shrill warbling sound from outside.

"Uh-oh!" said Meep, putting his paws over his ears.

"What's that noise?" asked Priti.

"It's Lottie," said Zoe. "I'd better go and make sure she's OK." She hurried outside to see Lottie running in a circle around the zebras.

Cleo gave a loud whinny and Theo stamped his front foot crossly. They clearly didn't like Lottie crowding them, even though she was very small and only trying to be friendly.

"Come here, Lottie," said Zoe, putting the little llama back on her lead. She was worried the zebras might get cross and kick Lottie. "The zebras need to go to sleep soon."

Lottie sighed and looked sad.

While Priti held Lottie on her lead, Zoe helped Great-Uncle Horace place thick woolly blankets over the zebras' backs.

"Now they'll be nice and snug for the night," said Great-Uncle Horace.

They left the stable, carefully shutting the door behind them, and made their

way from the enclosure.

It was now snowing so heavily Zoe could barely see.

"Will Lottie be OK out in the garden in this?" she asked. "Her shelter isn't completely enclosed and it's so cold!"

Great-Uncle Horace frowned. "No, I think we need to find her another shelter for the night."

"But where?" asked Zoe. She was nervous about putting Lottie in with any of the other animals. She was just too eager and bouncy! And Zoe's cosy cottage didn't have enough room for a bouncing llama.

"I know just the place," said Great-Uncle Horace thoughtfully. "Follow me!"

Chapter Six
Llama Sleepover!

"Where are we going?" asked Zoe as she ran to keep up with Great-Uncle Horace's long-legged strides.

"Somewhere dry and warm, where we can toast crumpets on the fire," replied Great-Uncle Horace mysteriously, with a twinkle in his eye.

"Do you know where he means?" Priti

asked Zoe.

"Yes, I think so," replied Zoe with a grin.

They followed the path until the hill at the back of the zoo came into view. Up on top of the hill was a grand old manor house. Lights blazed from the windows and across the snow.

"Higgins Hall!" exclaimed Zoe.

"Yes, indeed," replied Great-Uncle Horace.

"It's where Great-Uncle Horace lives," Zoe explained to Priti. "And quite a few animals live there too!"

Higgins Hall had belonged to Great-Uncle Horace's family for over a hundred years, but ever since Horace had built the Rescue Zoo he used most of the rooms to house different animals. He stayed in the attic at the very top of the house whenever he was back home.

The girls and Lottie and Meep followed Great-Uncle Horace up the hill to the house. It was painted bright green, with a brass knocker in the shape of a fox's head in the middle. Great-Uncle Horace took a huge bunch of keys from his coat pocket. The door creaked loudly as he opened it.

As they stepped inside there was a flutter of blue feathers and Kiki flew down from the chandelier hanging in the centre of the entrance hall to perch on his shoulder.

"Hello, Kiki. We have a special guest come to stay the night." Great-Uncle Horace patted Lottie on the head and the little llama hummed happily.

"I think I'm going to put our special

guest in the conservatory," said Great-Uncle Horace thoughtfully, heading over to one of the many doors leading off the hall.

They followed him into the living room. It was full of elegant furniture but the carpet was faded and frayed. A bat hung, fast asleep, from the light! Great-Uncle Horace led Lottie into a conservatory at the back of the house. It had a stone floor and tall windows and looked just the right place for a llama to have a sleepover!

"Make yourselves at home." He smiled. "I'll just let your mum know where we are, Zoe, and ask her to join us for tea. Then I'll fetch some hay and food and water for Lottie." He went over to an old-fashioned phone on a table by the fireplace and picked up the receiver.

By the time Lucy arrived, Great-Uncle Horace had lit a fire in the fireplace and Zoe and Priti were toasting crumpets on long forks over the flames. Lottie was dozing in the conservatory and Meep was curled up on the sofa, fast asleep.

Looking at Meep sleeping peacefully gave Zoe an idea.

"Could Priti and I stay in Higgins Hall tonight?" She looked at Lucy and Great-Uncle Horace hopefully.

"I don't see why not," replied Lucy. "If it's OK with Uncle Horace."

"The more the merrier!" boomed Great-Uncle Horace. "We could set up a couple of camp beds on the floor."

Priti and Zoe hugged each other excitedly.

"Best. Sleepover. Ever!" exclaimed Priti.

The next morning, Zoe woke to a weird squeaking sound. She rubbed her eyes sleepily but, no, she wasn't still asleep and dreaming. Lottie really was trotting up and down in front of the fireplace with

Meep riding on her back! The little lemur clapped his front paws and squeaked excitedly.

"Meep, what are you doing?" giggled Zoe.

In the camp bed next to her, Priti stretched and yawned. When she saw Lottie and Meep she started laughing too. "It's so much fun having a sleepover with animals," she said. "And I think they're having just as much fun as us!"

A loud knocking came from the hall.

"There's someone at the door," said Zoe. She got out of bed and went to answer it. Lucy was standing on the doorstep, wrapped up warm in her coat, woolly hat and scarf, holding a big bag. Everything outside was covered in a thick blanket of snow.

"Morning, Mum. Wow, look at the snow!" exclaimed Zoe as Priti, Lottie and Meep gathered round her at the door.

"Morning, girls, how did you sleep?" said Lucy, coming inside and stamping the snow from her boots.

"Great, thanks," replied Zoe.

"I wish we didn't have to go to school," said Priti with a sigh.

"Then your wish has come true." Lucy smiled.

"What do you mean?" asked Zoe.

"I just got a message from your school. It snowed heavily in the night and the boiler isn't working, so they're not going to be opening today. I've spoken to Priti's mum and it's fine for her to spend the day here with us."

"It's a snow day!" cried Zoe happily.

But then she remembered something. "Oh! But the rest of the class are meant to be coming to the zoo to rehearse with the animals. It's the school winter show tomorrow, and we really need to practise. So many people are coming to watch us!" Zoe suddenly had butterflies in her tummy at the thought of everyone coming to see the show without it being ready. It could be a disaster!

"I'll speak to Miss Hawkins and try to work something out," said Lucy. "Leave it with me!"

After breakfast Zoe and Priti wrapped up warm, put on their boots and set off into the zoo with Lottie, Meep and Great-Uncle Horace. The zoo hadn't opened yet so the snow was still fresh and untrodden. The girls had great fun making patterns with their footprints, even though they were both still feeling a bit anxious about not being able to practise for the show with their school friends and the animals.

As they walked past the penguin enclosure, they saw Mr Pinch stomping towards them. As usual, he was wearing his extra-smart zoo manager's uniform but with a big pair of wellington boots.

"Good morning, Mr Pinch," called Zoe.

"What's so good about it?" grumbled Mr Pinch. "The zoo has turned into the North Pole overnight."

"But it looks so lovely," said Zoe.

"Hmm, until it turns to slush," muttered Mr Pinch. "Anyway, I can't stand around talking all day. I have paths to clear."

"Don't worry about him," Zoe whispered to Priti as Mr Pinch stomped off through the snow. "He's really grumpy on the outside but he can be quite nice . . . sometimes."

Just then Zoe heard the sound of excited voices coming down the path. She couldn't believe her eyes when she saw her whole class coming towards her, led by Miss Hawkins!

"The school heating system has broken, so school will be closed for a few days," said Miss Hawkins.

"But what about the show tomorrow?" cried Zoe. "If school is closed we won't be able to use the hall!"

"Don't worry, Zoe," smiled Great-Uncle Horace, coming to join the group with Kiki perched on the shoulder of his thick winter coat. "I've told Miss Hawkins she is welcome to put the show on here at the zoo – the marquee will be big enough and we can all work together today to get it spruced up and ready!"

Zoe, Priti and the rest of the class, snug in their wellies, warm coats, hats and gloves, cheered happily.

Zoe couldn't believe it. She got to spend the day with all her friends and the zoo animals AND the show would go ahead at the zoo. This was the best school day ever!

Zoe and her classmates had a very busy day. Not only did they help to tidy and put the chairs in the marquee and decorate it with fairy lights and Christmas decorations, but they spent lots of time with the wintry animals and their keepers. Zoe and the zoo keepers helped teach Zoe's classmates even more fun facts about the animals they'd been paired with!

Miss Hawkins had a surprise for Great-Uncle Horace to say thank you for all his help. She gave him a special guest role as a snowman who would welcome the audience and introduce the show! But the BEST news about the amazing snowy rehearsal day was that Great-Uncle Horace received a call about a new llama needing a home, so he was going to go and collect her right away! Soon Lottie would have a herd of her very own.

Chapter Seven
Show Time!

When Zoe woke up on the morning of
the show, the first thing she did was look
out of the window. She breathed a sigh of
relief. There was a blanket of snow on the
ground, just enough to make the zoo look
magical but not so much that it would
have stopped the guests from coming to
see the show!

"Morning, Mum! It's show day!" she exclaimed as she bounded into the kitchen.

"Morning, love." Lucy was looking at her phone. "I'm afraid I have a bit of bad news."

Zoe's heart sank. "What is it?"

"I've just heard from Great-Uncle Horace. Something unexpected has come up with the llama he's rescuing, so he's not going to be able to make it back in time for the show."

"What's happened?" Zoe sat down at the table feeling really sad.

"I'm not sure. He didn't say in his message," replied Lucy, giving Zoe a hug.

Zoe felt really glum. Lottie might not be getting a new friend *and* there would be no one to play the snowman in the show either.

After Zoe had finished her breakfast
and done her chores, she put Lottie on her
lead and set off with Meep to meet her
classmates and get ready for the show.

As she reached the green in the middle
of the zoo she stopped to look at the
marquee. It looked amazing! Fairy lights
twinkled all around it and a big banner
that Zoe and her classmates had made
saying "WELCOME TO OUR WINTER
SHOW!" hung over the entrance.

Sally from the café had set up a stall
beside the marquee, where she was going
to be selling hot chocolate and roast
chestnuts. But even the delicious smells
coming from the stall couldn't cheer Zoe
up. To make matters worse, Mr Pinch was
busy sweeping snow from the footpath. He
was bound to be in a bad mood.

"Good morning, Zoe!" he called when he saw her.

Zoe stared at him in shock. He actually seemed happy! And for once she was the one in the bad mood. "Good morning, Mr Pinch," she said quietly.

Mr Pinch stopped sweeping. "Is everything all right, Zoe?"

Zoe sighed. "Great-Uncle Horace has had a problem with the llama he was supposed to be rescuing so he won't be back in time for the school show. So we've got no one to play the snowman."

Meep started bouncing around Mr Pinch's feet and pulling at the bottom of his trousers.

"What on earth is that creature doing?" said Mr Pinch with a frown, trying to shake Meep off.

"Him, him, him!" chattered Meep.

Zoe's eyes lit up as she realised what Meep was trying to say. "Er, Mr Pinch, would you mind being the snowman for us? All you have to do is welcome everyone to the show – and, er, wear the snowman costume." Zoe held her breath. There was probably no way Mr Pinch would agree to dressing up as a snowman – he loved wearing his uniform too much. But, to her surprise, he nodded.

"All right."

"What?" Zoe stared at him in shock.

"I'll do it." Then Mr Pinch started humming a tune.

"Are you OK, Mr Pinch? You seem very – happy."

"Do I?" For a moment Mr Pinch looked confused. "Well, I suppose I am happy. I had a phone call from your teacher this morning. All the tickets for the show have been snapped up, which means we'll be having lots of visitors today ... which means they'll be spending lots of money in the zoo."

Zoe grinned. The one thing that was guaranteed to make Mr Pinch happy was the thought of

more money for the zoo! Zoe heard the honk of a horn and turned to see the school minibus pulling up by the marquee – her classmates were here!

The children went backstage to practise their lines and change into their costumes. An hour later the audience began to take their seats. Then, ten minutes before the show was due to begin, the keepers came backstage with the animals who were starring in the show!

Zoe knew they were all very excited. Holly, Snowy and Ivy, the snow leopard cubs, were particularly energetic and kept getting their special leads tangled up as they played and explored. Matt certainly had his hands full! Lottie was enjoying being backstage with all the children and trying to keep them all together using her super herding skills.

Mr Pinch had put on the snowman's costume and was practising his lines. Zoe felt a nervous fluttering in her tummy.

She really hoped the show would go well. Finally the audience fell silent – it was show time!

Mr Pinch walked out on to the stage. "Welcome, everyone, to the Rescue Zoo and the school's winter performance. I really hope you enjoy the show!"

One by one, the five different groups of children took to the stage to tell the audience all about special wintry places in the world and some of the amazing animals that lived in those environments.

The animals went on stage with the children too, so everyone could see them. The performances went very well, and the guests – who filled the marquee – clapped after each section and cheered quietly so as not to upset the animals. Zoe's llama group was the last to go on.

The audience all gasped when they saw Zoe and her friends wearing their home-made llama ears and costumes and leading little Lottie!

"This is Lottie the llama," announced Zoe, patting her on the head. Lottie gave a friendly hum.

"Lottie is the latest animal to find a home at the Rescue Zoo," said Priti. "Her wild relatives live in South America: in Argentina, Bolivia, Chile and Peru."

"Llamas are specially adapted to life

high up in the mountains," added Zoe. "They have thick fur to protect them from the cold . . ." Priti stood next to Lottie here, showing off her beautiful coat to the audience. ". . . and their feet have two toes and leathery soles, to protect them from the sharp rocks."

"They belong to the camelid family, who lived in North America forty million years ago!" said Alfie.

"And a baby llama, like Lottie, is called a cria," added Charlie.

"*And* llamas are great at carrying loads!" finished Zoe, winking at Meep. The tiny lemur stood up on Lottie's back as she started trotting around the stage. The audience all clapped and cheered as the four children proudly led Lottie and Meep offstage.

Now that everyone had performed their piece and introduced their animals, it was time for the final group song. The children led all of the animals on to the stage, with the zoo keepers by their sides.

But before they could start singing there was a loud *THUD* from outside as a big clump of frozen snow slid off the marquee and hit the floor. Oscar the snowy owl and his mate Shelley screeched loudly, flapped their wings and took to the air in fright. This loud noise and sudden movement made Pip and her two penguin friends scared, and they squawked and waddled to the front of the stage. Piper the puffin tried to hide and tripped keeper Rory over, who in turn knocked Matt over. The big-cat keeper let go of the snow leopards' leads in the confusion.

The three snow leopard cubs, Holly, Snowy and Ivy, were very excited by all the commotion and scampered off the stage purring happily, their leads trailing behind them.

"Come back!" cried Zoe. But it was too late. The cubs ran off towards the exit, followed closely by the penguins and puffins! Then Lottie gave a loud bray and trotted off after them. Oscar and Shelley started to swoop around the marquee, hooting loudly.

"Oh no!" cried Zoe as the little llama trotted over to the stairs, with Meep still on her back. "Now Lottie's escaping too!"

"Animal emergency!" Mr Pinch yelled from inside his snowman's suit, struggling to remove the big round head of the costume.

The audience gasped in shock and ducked in their seats as the owls swooped overhead and the animals raced down the aisle towards the back of the marquee. Lottie was at the back of the group. To Zoe's astonishment, when Lottie reached the penguins and puffins she gently nudged the little birds with her nose and hummed softly. Pip put his head on one side and then squawked to Pearl and Poppy. The three penguins then turned and waddled back to the stage! Piper and her puffin pals followed closely behind, as Lottie hummed reassuringly to them all and nudged them softly with her nose.

Next, Lottie bounced after the three snow leopard cubs, managing to get in front of them. Making soft humming sounds and with her ears pricked forward, she trotted in a circle around them, keeping them together and preventing them from getting too close to the exit.

"She's trying to herd them!" exclaimed Zoe. But would the cubs let Lottie guide them back to their keeper? Lottie wasn't much bigger than the cubs and they

seemed very overexcited and full of mischief.

Lottie brayed loudly at the three cubs again and stamped her hoof firmly. Yowling softly, the cubs paused for a moment and then turned round and started running back up the aisle towards

Matt, who had untangled himself from
the other keepers on the stage. The
audience started to cheer. Soon the cubs
were back with Matt and enjoying a
meaty treat, while Oscar and Shelley
were calmly perched on their keeper's
shoulder.

Zoe gave Lottie a big hug. "Well done,"
she whispered in the little llama's ear.
"That was the best herding I've ever seen!
You may only be little, but you have a
very big, brave heart!"

The little llama hummed proudly and
nuzzled Zoe's hand.

The children and animals all took their
places again to sing the final song. When
they'd finished, the audience leapt to their
feet and gave an extra-loud cheer. The
animals all squawked and chirped and

yowled happily and the children bowed. Mr Pinch gave such a big bow he almost toppled over!

After the animals had been safely taken back to their enclosures, Zoe left the marquee with her friends, holding Lottie on her lead. Christmassy songs were playing from speakers outside the gift shop and people were queuing to buy hot chocolates and chestnuts from Sally on her stall. Zoe smiled. The show had been a huge success – and Lottie had saved the day! She patted the llama on the head. It was such a shame Great-Uncle Horace had missed it.

But then she heard the musical tune of a car horn and she turned to see Great-Uncle Horace's car pulling up beside the marquee. The trailer was attached to it –

had he managed to bring back another llama?

"Hello, everybody!" boomed Great-Uncle Horace as he got out of the car. "Zoe, I'm so sorry I missed the show. How did it go?"

"It was great!" exclaimed Zoe. "And Lottie was the star." She quickly told him what had happened and how Lottie had come to the rescue, stopping all of the other animals from escaping into the snow!

"That's wonderful!" said Great-Uncle Horace. "And I have some more good news."

"Have you rescued another llama?" asked Zoe eagerly.

"No. . ." he replied.

Zoe's heart sank. That would have been

the perfect ending to the day.

"You'd better take a look for yourself," said Great-Uncle Horace. He opened the door of the trailer ... and as Zoe peered in she saw not one but *two* pairs of dark-brown eyes! One of the llamas was fully grown but the other was a tiny baby!

"Oh my goodness!" exclaimed Zoe. "We have two new llamas for the zoo?"

"Yes! It turns out that the llama I was rescuing was pregnant," explained Great-Uncle Horace. "That's why I got held up. I had to help deliver this one." He carefully helped the baby llama down from the trailer. Its woolly coat was extra fluffy and it legs were thin and wobbly. The baby's mum jumped down and stood next to it.

Lottie hummed excitedly and went over

to nuzzle them.

The mummy llama hummed back and the baby gave an excited squeak. The three llamas stood together happily, noses touching, the snow glistening around them.

Zoe couldn't stop grinning. This really was the best day ever. The show had gone brilliantly *and* Lottie the little llama finally had friends and a very special herd of her very own!

Zoe's Rescue Zoo

Look out for MORE amazing animal adventures at the Rescue Zoo!

The Secret Rescuers

If you enjoyed this book,
we think you'll love The Secret Rescuers!

Look out for another AMAZING series from Nosy Crow!